Copyright © 1996 by Nord-Süd Verlag AG, Gossau Zürich, Switzerland
First published in Switzerland under the title *Die Besucher-Sucher*
English translation copyright © 1996 by North-South Books Inc.

First published in the United States, Great Britain, Canada,
Australia, and New Zealand in 1996 by North-South Books,
an imprint of Nord-Süd Verlag AG, Gossau Zürich, Switzerland.

Distributed in the United States by North-South Books Inc., New York.

Library of Congress Cataloging-in-Publication Data is available.
A CIP catalogue record for this book is available from The British Library.
ISBN 1-55858-554-0 (trade binding)
1 3 5 7 9 TB 10 8 6 4 2
ISBN 1-55858-555-9 (library binding)
1 3 5 7 9 LB 10 8 6 4 2
Printed in Germany

The Friendship Trip

WRITTEN AND ILLUSTRATED BY

Wolfgang Slawski

Translated by Rosemary Lanning

North-South Books / New York / London

In a big station, in a big city,
trains from near and far came
and went all day long.

And all day long a man in a checked cap sat on a bench and watched the trains coming and going. He watched people saying hello and good-bye, greeting visitors and seeing them off.

Whenever a train pulled in, the man
in the checked cap, whose name was
Arthur, stood up to see if someone had
come to visit him. But no one ever came.
When the train pulled out again, he
was still alone.

One day Arthur had an idea. "I'm waiting at the wrong station!" he decided. "People coming to visit me must think I'm somewhere else." He bought a ticket, jumped on a train, and hurried off to the next town to see what would happen there.

When Arthur got off the train, he met another man
with a cap. Arthur sat down next to him and asked,
"Has anyone come here looking for me?"

"No," said the man with the cap. "Nor for me either,
I'm sad to say. No one ever gets off here."

"Perhaps this is the wrong station too," said Arthur.
"Let's give the next one a try."

"Good idea," said the other man, and off they went.

At the next station
they met a woman who
told them she had never
had any visitors either.

"Why don't you come
with us?" suggested Arthur.
"We're looking for a station
where people do come to
visit you."

The woman was happy
to join them.

As their journey went
on, more and more people
tagged along.

Soon there was no room
on the station benches for
everyone to sit and wait.
So they brought their
own chairs.

Before long
there was hardly
enough room on the
station platforms
for them all
to stand.

And finally there were
enough passengers to fill a
small town. Arthur couldn't
believe how many other people
had been waiting for someone
to visit them.

The train journeyed far and wide. Then one day Arthur realized there wasn't a single place they hadn't visited.

"What do we do now?" he asked the man with the cap. "We've been everywhere, but we still haven't met anyone who was coming to visit us."

"You're quite right," said the man with the cap.

They stopped the train and everyone stood around
wondering what to do.

   "I've got it!" cried Arthur. "We can visit each other.
After all, we're friends now."

   "Of course!" said the man with the cap. "I'll send you
an invitation."

   "And I'll send one to you," said Arthur.

That night all the passengers had a party,
with good food and music and bright
paper lanterns swaying overhead. They
laughed and sang and made plans to visit
each other when they all got home.